THE REAL GHOSTBUSTERS™

Drool
the Dog-Faced Goblin

Adapted by Maureen Spurgeon
from the original TV script
by Linda Woolverton

Egon Spengler was the only Ghostbuster who had any idea where they were going. Even Ray Stantz who was driving Ecto-1 was completely in the dark. And the further he drove, the more Peter Venkman moaned and groaned. Peter was never happy about leaving New York. He got withdrawal symptoms.

'I — I can feel my powers draining away . . . I'm fading . . . fading!' he kept wailing. 'Even Ecto-1 is weakening . . .'

There seemed to be some truth in that last remark. Ecto-1 was certainly making a lot of strange noises. Ray drove carefully on, following a line of giant yellow and green cardboard arrows, that pointed towards a delapidated group of tents and trailers.

Next minute, Ecto-1 shuddered and spluttered to

a halt. The Ghostbusters piled out impatiently.

'I told you!' cried Peter, with an air of triumph. 'We're too far away from New York City! It's draining our strength!'

They all looked round in silence. No one was very impressed with what he saw.

'*Madame Lafarge's Wondrous and Amazing Travelling Sideshow!*' Ray read from a forlorn-looking banner that waved feebly in the breeze.

'Egon,' Winston asked, 'exactly why are we here?'

'We're here,' replied Egon, pointing to a sign, 'to check that out! What do you think?'

'*See the Amazing Two-Headed Rabbit!*' Winston read aloud from a nearby sign. '*A Living Unicorn! A Real Mermaid! And Drool, the Dog-faced . . .*'

His words faltered to a stop, leaving the rest of The Ghostbusters to finish the sentence in tones of stunned disbelief.

'*Goblin?*'

'It's got to be a fake!' Peter pronounced at last. 'How could a sleazy place like this have a real goblin?'

There was no answer. As they stood around pondering this, a young woman approached them. She was dressed in colourful, theatrical clothes and had a mane of long, blonde hair. She stared at The Ghostbusters, expectantly.

'Er — you must be Madame Lafarge,' greeted Winston, thinking that somebody ought to say something. 'We're The Real Ghostbusters.'

'I've heard of you,' Madame Lafarge answered. She did not seem to be particularly impressed or interested. 'May I ask why you're here?'

'We're here to solve your goblin problem!' said Ray.

'That's very nice,' said Madame Lafarge, folding her arms crossly, 'but I don't have a goblin problem. And now,' she continued, 'if you don't mind, I have a show to put on.'

It wasn't much of a show. There was a two-headed rabbit who munched sadly on a piece of lettuce, a unicorn, which was really a goat with a fake horn attached to its forehead, and a mermaid, who was leaning over the edge of the water tank, filing her fingernails.

Most people were heading towards the biggest tent, so The Ghostbusters followed. This was obviously where all the action was.

'Look, folks,' Madame Lafarge was saying, 'see who we managed to coax out of retirement! It's Little Egypt!'

'Little Egypt?' echoed Peter, as an arm — rather a flabby arm — peeped out coyly from behind a tattered curtain, followed by a leg — rather a wobbly sort of leg — draped in muslin with lots of bracelets around the ankle. Little Egypt danced bravely round the stage jangling her bracelets and shaking her hair. Some of the audience tried hard not to giggle, but Ray was rather enjoying her performance — she reminded him of his grandmother.

Then, just as The Ghostbusters were wondering how they could leave without hurting her feelings, a bloodcurdling screech tore through the air. They could hardly believe it — but there, on stage, was a hideous, slobbering, four-armed, four-footed, slimy goblin.

A frenzy of screams and terrified yells immediately broke out as the horrified audience stampeded towards the exit. The Ghostbusters jumped to their feet, Proton Guns ready to fire.

'There really *is* a goblin!' gasped Winston, not bothering to wait for Egon to check his PKE meter. 'Surround it, you guys!'

'No!' screamed Madame Lafarge, at the very moment they were ready to shoot. 'Please don't fire those things at Drool! He's part of the show! Drool adopted us a couple of years ago,' she explained, gently ushering the goblin towards them.

Close up, they could see he had a wet, lopsided

grin and a droopy, wrinkled nose, making him look rather like a pet bloodhound.

'He's been tagging along ever since, and I finally put him in the show! Drool,' she continued, 'show these nice people what you can do!'

But The Ghostbusters had seen goblins change shape before. A ghostly-green skeleton . . . a green vampire bat . . . a huge, green caterpillar-worm . . . an enormous green spider . . . underneath it all there was the same fat, slobbering goblin.

'Come on, lady,' Peter burst out impatiently. 'Let's get him!'

But Madame Lafarge was not going to give in without a fight.

'Don't you think all this running around busting ghosts has made you guys a little trigger-happy?' she asked, her face creased with anger as she stepped forward to protect the goblin. 'Drool is perfectly harmless.'

The Ghostbusters were shamed into silence. They reluctantly lowered their Proton Guns and, shuffling awkwardly, they got back in Ecto-1 and drove away.

'I still think we should have busted that thing!' announced Peter.

'But what if Madame Lafarge is right?' Winston questioned reasonably. 'Maybe he is just a harmless four-footed goblin?'

All conversation came to a halt as a shower of sparks and flashes shot out into the deserted road behind them, followed by a succession of crashes and bangs. Ecto-1 had broken down completely. And this time, they were stranded, right in the middle of nowhere. Peter had had enough.

'Ecto-1, don't do this to me! I have to get back to New York! I – I'm getting weaker . . .'

'Peter!' snapped Ray warningly. 'Get pushing . . .'

But, even with all four Ghostbusters pushing, Ecto-1 wouldn't move. Everyone stared silently at the car, unaware that far above them, from the top of a telegraph pole, they were being watched . . .

Suddenly there was a dangerously loud crack, followed by a crash, as a power line swung heavily down, heading right towards Ray.

'Ray! Look out!' yelled Winston, leaping towards him and pulling him to safety. Another second and he would have been too late. The moment the power line hit the ground, it sparked and sizzled dangerously, wriggling perilously near Ray's feet.

'Ray!' panted Peter, still getting over the shock. 'You almost got yourself stir-fried!'

His words were almost drowned by a burst of evil, high-pitched laughter, followed by the noisy scurrying of someone – or *something* – moving through the bushes.

'What was that?' breathed Winston.

'If you ask me,' replied Peter, 'it looked very much like a certain goblin we all know . . .'

'Come on,' said Ray. 'Let's get Ecto-1 to a garage and then clear outta here!'

But when they finally found a garage, it was shut. There was only one thing for it – they would have to spend the night in this place and go home in the morning.

'No! No! No!' yelled Peter as they approached a hotel. 'You can't do this to me! I refuse to stay in some flea-bag boarding house.'

However even he was impressed when he saw his room. It was surprisingly clean and big. In fact, not bad at all.

In the room next door, Ray was settling down for the night when he was disturbed by the sound of a large dog barking outside his door.

'Stupid dog!' he mumbled, annoyed at having to get out of bed. 'Shut up!'

He threw the door open but, instead of a dog there was a kitten. Its tiny head was thrown back, but instead of meeowing, it was barking very loudly. Ray couldn't understand it, but he was too tired to work it all out. So, he shrugged his shoulders and climbed back into bed, looking forward to a good night's sleep.

But not for long. Just as he was about to snuggle down between the sheets, he heard a plaintive, 'Meee-ow!', right outside his door. Could it be the tiny kitten? He decided to check . . . There, on his doorstep was a huge great St Bernard. 'Meee-ow!' it cried out again.

Meanwhile Egon was sitting at a table in his room, working out some calculations. When there was a polite knock on his door, he thought it was room service with his coffee.

'Come on in!' he called. If he had glanced up, he would have seen what a very hairy-looking hand the waiter had. 'Just leave it on the desk. Thanks!'

One swallow later and Egon wished he hadn't bothered with a late night drink.

'Call this coffee?' he gagged, one hand clutched around his throat. 'It tastes like mud!'

Angrily he emptied the coffee out into his saucer.
It slopped out in one big, brown dollop. 'Oh, sorry!'
said Egon. 'It is mud.'

Winston was looking forward to a good night's
sleep. Entering his room, he threw down his proton
pack and kicked off his shoes. Sighing heavily with
exhaustion, he threw himself onto the bed.
KERTHUMP! He landed on the floor. Where had the
bed gone? *Of course* — there it was, floating in
mid-air, along with his shoes, proton pack and the
rest of the furniture. Where else would it be? And
now Winston was rising up to join them. What *was*
going on?

As for Peter — he had just found the shower.
Happily humming to himself, he reached over and
turned on the taps. 'AAAARRRRGGGGHHHH!' he
cried as he was plastered from head to foot with

something red and slippery. Tomato soup! He was covered in tomato soup.

The other Ghostbusters, hearing his cry, came hurrying into his room. 'You're covered in tomato soup,' said Ray who had a talent for stating the obvious. It was then that the vision of a green, four-footed goblin called Drool floated in front of Peter's soup-splattered eyes.

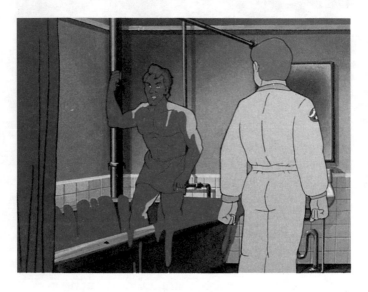

'I'm gonna get that little nerk!' he snarled.

That night The Ghostbusters had the full treatment . . . wails and groans, creaking doors, hollow footsteps, icy fingertips in the dark. It seemed like ages before the sun came up, and they could start thinking about getting back to New York.

But still their problems weren't over. As they stumbled out into the bright sunlight, there was suddenly a rumble of thunder, low and menacing. As they looked upwards, a storm of hail pelted their faces so hard that they all yelled with pain.

'That's not hail!' cried Egon, snatching a piece of 'hail' and putting it in his mouth. 'Ugh! It's dried sweetcorn!'

Winston had had enough. 'All right, you crummy green twerp!' he yelled up at the sky. 'Come on out and face us!'

The Ghostbusters took out their Proton Guns, ready to fire, but the hail stopped as suddenly as it began. An uncanny silence swirled all around them. Then, out of nowhere, came a gale-force wind, followed by a horrible, high-pitched scream. In the middle of all this chaos rose one of the ugliest spooks they had ever seen. He swooped towards them, his many heads twisting and turning, his teeth bared, ready for the kill.

Proton Beams shot out from four Proton Guns, but as fast as they hit one hideous-looking head, the monster sprouted another, then another, until it was impossible to hit them all.

'There's only one logical thing to do,' Egon yelled out to the others. 'RUN!'

They all teared down the street, the monster following, snapping and snarling behind them, until they reached a doorway. Sprinting inside they noticed that they had entered a laundry. Leaning against the counter they all tried to get their breath back.

'It's okay,' Ray panted to the man behind the

counter. 'We're scientists!'

'Oh yeah?' He was obviously not convinced. 'So, let me see an experiment — right now!'

Egon was about to demonstrate how his PKE meter operated, when he was interrupted by a revolting, slurping noise. The gruesome green ghoulie was smacking each of its hideous heads up against the window.

'Okay, you're scientists!' gasped the laundry man, hurriedly backing away. 'Never doubted it for a minute!'

The back door slammed shut. The Ghostbusters were left alone with the screeching fiend.

'Shoo!' cried Peter in desperation, waving his hands at it. 'Get away! Move it, Buster!'

The monster hesitated for a moment, then flew away! Egon was flabbergasted.

'It — it worked!' he stammered. 'It — it worked!'

'Of course,' said Peter nonchalantly. 'You have to show these things who's Boss!'

But none of them had noticed a strange, white mist oozing under the back door.

'So if you'll excuse me,' Peter continued, brushing the hanging laundry aside. 'I'm going out for a burger!'

If only he had had breakfast that morning! As he pushed aside one last steam-pressed suit, he found himself looking into the red, burning eyes of a tall, dark, hooded figure, which grinned at him with long, menacing fangs.

'AAAAGGGGHHHH!' screamed Peter, stumbling backwards into a great pile of laundry. The creature came slowly towards him, each footstep heavy with dread. Peter frantically struggled to get out of the pile of laundry. 'AAAAGGGGHHHH!' he yelled to the others. 'It's the thing . . . the monster . . . it's here. Only it's changed its shape . . .'

Next minute there was a hideous roar and the monster lunged towards the other Ghostbusters, scattering laundry everywhere as he did so.

'RUN!' they all yelled together.

'We — we can't keep running away from that

thing,' panted Winston, once they had scrambled inside a nearby empty warehouse. 'We've got to try and trap it somehow!'

'Yeah,' agreed Ray. 'What we need is some nice, juicy bait . . .'

'Uh-oh,' groaned Peter as the others turned to him, smiling in a revoltingly sickly way.

'You only have to keep the creature occupied while we move in from behind,' said Winston.

'You've got the easy job!' agreed Egon.

'That's nice,' said Peter sarcastically. 'For a moment there, I thought it was going to be dangerous!'

The others left Peter alone in the middle of the dark, empty warehouse. His voice echoed in the stillness, 'All I wanted was a nice little goblin to deal with . . .'

The only answer was a distant scratching noise. The sort of noise no one notices, until it comes closer . . . and closer . . until it is impossible to ignore.

'Okay, okay' Peter said to himself, standing very stiff, with his eyes tightly shut. 'Whatever it is, you

can handle it. You can handle anything . . .'

He opened his eyes, then wished he could shut them again, or fall to the ground, or turn around and start running — anything except just stand there. The monster had changed into a giant cockroach and it was scratching its way across the deserted warehouse towards him.

'Oh, no!' he yelled. 'Not that! Anything but that! I hate cockroaches.'

'We're coming' shouted Winston. 'Don't move.'

There was no chance of that. Peter was rooted to the spot, petrified with fear. Through the gloom, he could just about make out the other three Ghostbusters coming up behind the cockroach. When Egon had set up the Ghost Trap, Ray shouted the order.

'FIRE!'

Although they were all on target, it didn't seem to make any difference. The cockroach was still there, circling around Peter, its huge claws snapping in the air. Again and again The Ghostbusters fired, but it was no good. Plaster fell from the ceiling, windows shattered and walls crumbled, but still the cockroach kept moving.

Finally the cockroach trapped Peter in the corner and was rearing up on its hind legs, ready to pounce. This was just what the others had been waiting for. They began to close in still firing their Proton Guns. This new onslaught seemed to be too much for the cockroach. The creature squeezed itself into the crack between the floor and the wall, and vanished out of sight. There was a general sigh of relief, then Ray asked what they had all been thinking, 'Now, what do we do?'

'How do we capture something that keeps changing shape?' asked Winston. 'I kind of wish it was that Drool goblin thing. Then, at least we'd know what we're dealing with!'

'Why can't it be him?' Peter broke in. 'He

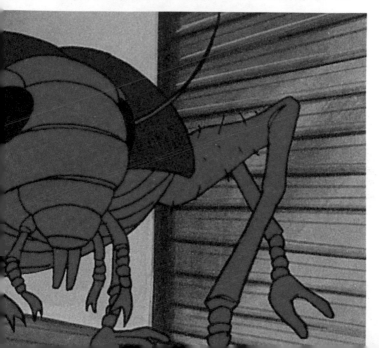

changed forms while we were with Madame Lafarge, didn't he?'

Egon was not convinced. 'Yes, but this monster registers about fifty times more Psycho Kinetic Energy on the PKE meter than the goblin did!'

'This is like last week when we couldn't catch that shape-changer,' Ray reflected. 'Remember him? The ghost that got away.'

'Well,' said Peter grimly, 'we're not going to let this one get away! Come on!' He started to sprint off in the direction of Ecto-1.

'We'll go back to the Sideshow,' yelled Ray, 'and bust the goblin when he goes home.'

'I still think you're way off course on this one, guys!' Egon told them, shaking his head. But nobody would listen.

They had all forgotten that Ecto-1 was still

broken down. But a little thing like that wasn't going to defeat Ray Stantz. A good kick with his boot, a turn of the ignition and the engine spluttered into life. Peter and Winston cheered and then climbed in.

'What do you call that, Ray?' Peter asked, grinning at him from the back seat.

'Something I forgot to try before,' Ray confessed. 'It's what's known as a kick start!'

Ecto-1 behaved perfectly all the way back to Madame Lafarge's Travelling Sideshow. The lady herself was there to greet them as they skidded to a stop outside the big tent.

'May I ask what you're doing here?' she asked them angrily.

'We've come to bust your favourite goblin!' Peter told her sharply. 'Drool's been a very naughty boy.

So, if you'll just step aside . . .'

'But . . . Drool is our friend!' she protested wildly. 'He wouldn't harm a hair on a human's head!'

'We're sure that your goblin is more than he appears to be,' said Peter, making his way into the tent. Winston followed him, but catching the sad look on Madame Lafarge's face, he stopped for a moment.

'Sorry,' he said quietly, 'but we've got to bust him!'

Madame Lafarge turned to Egon, her eyes

brimming with tears. 'Are *you* going to let them do this?'

'Well,' said Egon, wishing he didn't feel quite so cowardly about turning away, 'it *is* a goblin, after all.'

Inside the tent, Peter, Winston and Ray already had Drool cornered. He was shaking and shivering all over with fright.

'Maaooplooo?' he quavered in goblin language. 'Magoopla?'

'You know,' said Ray, his heart softening, 'he does look pretty harmless.'

'Yeah,' agreed Winston. 'He's really scared.'

'That's all an act!' said Peter, taking aim with his Proton Gun. The memories of all that had happened that day were still in his mind, especially the bit when he had been terrorised by the cockroach. 'Don't trust him for a second.'

The Ghostbusters blasted poor old Drool. Their four Proton Guns hit him at once, holding him in their rays ready to be sucked into the Ghost Trap that Egon had ready. But at that exact moment Madame Lafarge came charging into the tent, shrieking with terror.

'Help! Help! There's a . . . hor . . horrible thing outside! It's got . . . some . . . of . . . my people!'

'Sure, lady,' Peter nodded grimly, his Proton Gun still aimed on Drool, 'trying to distract us, eh?'

But then he started to hear frightened screaming

coming from outside, followed by some very familiar hideous screeches. And if he still had any doubts, they disappeared when a vicious gale force wind ripped the tent from its moorings and sent it crashing to the ground.

There was the monster, in all its revolting, repulsive glory, shrieking at the Sideshow people, who it had trapped between two trailers. Its gigantic heads were lunging at them, its huge tongues lashing out and all the while it was making a noise like four thousand finger nails screeching down a blackboard.

As one man, The Ghostbusters charged after him, Proton Guns at the ready. For the time being Drool was safe.

'Wait a minute,' bellowed Winston. 'If that's not Drool, then it must be him! The shape-changer that got away last week! It's got to be the same one. He's been following us ever since, waiting to strike back!'

'Move away,' Peter yelled to the people. 'That thing's dangerous!'

But which ever way the Sideshow people moved, the monster simply reached out a long tentacle and stopped them. Once or twice, Peter raised his Proton Gun, but he knew how easily the people could be hit if he fired.

At first, nobody saw Drool squeezing underneath the tent, running along on all four hands and feet. Then suddenly there he was — bravely standing in front of his friends from the Sideshow, baring his teeth at the monster like a well-trained guard dog. The monster lashed out again but this time, Drool

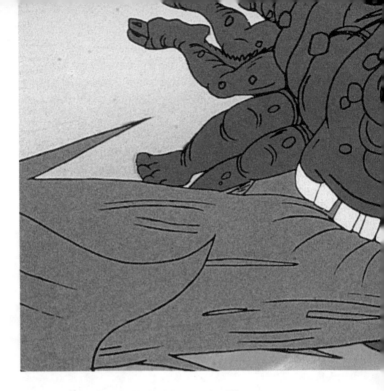

caught his tentacle in his teeth. The monster
yowled with pain.

'Let go, Drool!' yelled Winston as The
Ghostbusters raised their Proton Guns. 'You're in
the line of fire!'

'He can't!' Peter shouted. 'If he let's go, those
people have had it!'

Drool was clutching the tentacle with two of his
arms and looked over the top with his large, sad
eyes. He was nodding slowly.

'Mardock . . .' he murmured softly. 'Madoola
mee . . .'

Winston turned to Madame Lafarge.

'What did he say?' he asked.

'He says to save them,' her voice was wobbling with emotion. 'Do what you have to do.'

She had barely spoken, when the monster gave one last, desperate surge towards the Sideshow people. Everyone could see that Drool was only just holding it back.

'Mardock!' he shrieked out. 'Mardooooooock!'

The Ghostbusters glanced helplessly at each other, before taking aim with their Proton Guns.

'Buddy,' said Peter softly. 'I take it all back.'

Another minute, and both the monster and Drool were hit by the Proton Beams, Drool bravely hung

on to the horrible creature and they were
both sucked into the Ghost Trap together. The
monster was gone forever, but nobody was
celebrating. There were no cheers, no applause.
Instead The Ghostbusters had to face Madame
Lafarge. She stared at the Ghost Trap, watching the
red light flash on and off, her eyes misted up with
tears.

'We'll miss Drool,' she said. 'He was a loyal
friend. All of us are proud to have known him.'

'We'll put him in the Containment Unit back at
The Ghostbusters' HQ,' Ray told her. 'He'll be
among his own kind, so maybe he'll be happy
there.'

This idea seemed to bring some comfort to her,
and she turned away from them and walked slowly
over towards her trailer.

'I guess that's why he tagged along in the first place,' she said, half to herself. 'He wanted friends. Well, he sure found some here. We will always remember him.'

Ray and Peter looked at each other thoughtfully, and then down at the flashing light on the Containment Unit. For them it was a sign that Drool, the Dog-faced Goblin was where he belonged, at last.

Carnival
An imprint of the Children's Division
of the Collins Publishing Group
8 Grafton Street, London W1X 3LA

Published by Carnival 1989
Reprinted 1989

ISBN 0 00 194918 7

Printed and bound in Great Britain by
PURNELL BOOK PRODUCTION LIMITED
A member of BPCC plc